One Last Summer

PIPER RAYNE

Cover Design: By Hang Le

1st Line Editor: Joy Editing

2nd Line Editor: My Brother's Editor

Proofreader: My Brother's Editor

About One Last Summer

He's my first love. My high school sweetheart. And he's leaving tomorrow for a bigger and better life.

I've loved Ben almost my entire life, and we have one night left before he heads miles away to college on a football scholarship. I'm bound and determined to make sure this day goes perfectly so he remembers me as the girl he loves. But I can't help worrying that I'll end up as the girl he lov*ed*.

ONE LAST
Summer

Chapter One

BEN

I t's going to be weird not being here.

That's all I can think of standing on the front porch of my family's cattle ranch, looking out at our expansive land. This town, this land, this home are all I've known my entire life. Eighteen years of memories, good and bad. From racing my brothers home at dusk after a filled day of exploration, to my mom dying.

I'm excited to attend Clemson. But the elation is tempered by fear and worry because I'm leaving behind everybody I love.

I sigh.

The screen door slams shut on the wood frame.

"Jesus, are you really sulking that you leave tomorrow? Do you know how much pussy you're gonna pull at Clemson?"

I roll my eyes at my youngest brother, Emmett. He's fifteen and ruled by hormones.

"You wouldn't get it."

"What's to be sad about? You got a full ride to play football which makes you a hero in this town. And bonus, you're getting the hell outta Dodge. What's the downside?"

"Gillian—"

"Will be a distant memory once you get to South Carolina and meet all the fresh meat."

He's shot up in the last couple of months, almost meeting my six foot two inches now. Though at two hundred pounds, I have him out-muscled.

"You talk about girls like they're one of our heifers and you're the bull."

He shrugs. "Sorry, I don't put them on a pedestal like you do with Gillian."

"Keep Gillian out of it." My words hold a bite I don't intend. The last thing I want is to get into it with my brother, but today is my last day with Gillian before I leave, and I want every minute to be memorable.

Almost everyone else attending college, still has weeks before they have to leave, but football starts early for workouts and practice.

Emmett raises his hands. His classic move after he's the cause of my annoyance from his oversharing mouth. "You'll see soon enough."

"Where's Jude?" I ask.

My older brother, Jude is one year older than me but acts a decade older. Responsible, reliable, and grumpy are the three adjectives to describe him. It wasn't always that way though. Before my mom died, he was more carefree and wilder. Maybe he was always going to be the most responsible one of us three. Hard to say since we were only five and six when she died.

"Heard him tell Dad he was heading out to check a fence on the north end of the ranch."

A sharp familiar pain pinches my chest.

Guilt.

I'm leaving to play football and Jude's stuck here helping my dad run the ranch.

"What are you up to today?" Emmett jumps up on the porch railing.

"Picking up Gillian to swim at the old quarry and then coming back here."

Emmett's eyes light up. "Can I come?"

"Hell no."

My brother is the town's biggest flirt and the last thing me or Gillian want is to spend our last day together with my little brother in tow picking up girls. It's the reason I didn't invite my friends. I'll see everyone tonight at our annual Fourth of July pig roast, but this morning is just for us.

"You suck."

"Whatever." I walk across the porch to the wooden screen door and head inside.

The door slams against the wooden jamb making the same sound I've heard a thousand times in my life, but still, I stop to commit it to memory.

My dad's bedroom door is wide open as usual. He's shrugging on a clean T-shirt, wearing only a pair of boxer briefs. In a house full of only guys none of us feel the need to close the doors if we're changing.

"Hey, Dad."

He smiles, pride shining through the creases around his eyes. No one is happier about me playing college ball than him.

"You need me?" He walks over to his beat-up dresser, the same one he shared with my mom and pulls out a pair of jeans.

"Still okay if I take the truck this morning?"

"Yep. Just be back early afternoon. Gonna need your help before everyone arrives."

Willowbrook is a small town, and almost everyone ends up here at some point during the day to eat, hang out and trade stories we've all heard a hundred times.

"Will do. You need me to do anything before I go?"

A part of me hopes that he'll say yes. My dad has always required less of me than my brother's as far as the ranch goes,

3

insisting I concentrate on football. I wonder at times what he saw in me that he didn't in my brothers. As if he put all his eggs in my basket to make it out of this town.

He shakes his head. "Nah, we're good. Got Jude on what's needed done this morning."

There's that guilt sliding through my veins once more.

"Okay then, see you later."

"Later, son."

I grab the keys from the brass hook with a silhouette of a cow and the words, "I'm an expert in the field". I leap off the stairs to our scratched and dented red pickup truck parked in the dirt drive.

Gillian doesn't live too far from me, about fifteen minutes, but she's closer to town than me. She's already waiting outside when I pull up in front of her ramshackle bungalow.

She always waits outside when she's eager to get out of there.

One of the first things that bonded us when we met was that we were raised by single dads. First, her mom died during childbirth. Then her dad remarried but her stepmom ran off a couple years ago, which means Gillian's been picking up the slack at home with her two younger siblings Rowan and Koa.

Before I press on the truck's brakes, Gillian's walking my way. She whips open the passenger door and climbs inside.

"Rough morning?" I ask.

"You could say that." She sets her large beach bag at her feet and leans, giving me a chaste kiss.

Gillian attempts to pull away, but I place my palm to her face to keep her lips against mine. Her eyes are red-rimmed and swollen.

"Hey?"

She shakes her head. "Let's just enjoy our day together, okay?"

I study her face for a beat and nod. She doesn't add the

word last to her sentence, but I know she's thinking it. We both are.

She's been emotional about my leaving and despite my best efforts to reassure her she has nothing to worry about, that we're going to be fine, I still get the feeling that she thinks this impending goodbye is final.

I'll just have to prove her wrong.

Chapter Two

GILLIAN

The warm air streams into the truck's open cab windows on the way toward the old quarry. My eyes can't stop fixating on his hands on the steering wheel, the smell of the old pickup where we've made out for hours, not wanting to say goodbye late at night. I'd never tell him how I laid awake last night scared how I'll survive this town without him.

When he insisted I choose what we do today, I wasn't sure how to best spend our last day together until his Christmas break. It's a given that we'll end up at Plain Daisy Ranch at the end of the day, everyone does. I considered hanging around the ranch before the entire town showed up or taking a couple of the horses and hitting a trail for a picnic.

Then I remembered all the fun times we had throughout high school at the quarry and it felt right. That's how I want Ben to remember me while he's gone, a fun-loving, happy girl. Not the sullen and sad girl I've been repressing lately.

I can barely hear Carrie Underwood sing about heartbreak on the radio over the sound of the wind funneling through the truck. Which is probably a good thing, otherwise I'd be a crying mess. He mindlessly reaches over for my hand, gripping it in his large one. I've never felt safer than in this truck with him by my side. Now, he'll be ripped away from me like my childhood security blanket and I want to fall down and wail, but I'm putting on a brave face because he deserves the amazing opportunity of playing college football.

I look over at him and my heart does that thing it always does when I study him, it skips a few beats and then picks up the pace.

He's so good-looking with his soft brown eyes and matching hair. His hard, muscled body might intimidate some, but his baby face makes him more endearing.

Sometimes I can't believe he's mine, that he chose me. I'm not the head cheerleader, hell I'm not even a cheerleader at all. I was much happier keeping to myself.

Unlike him, I don't have a bright future ahead of me.

That's not to say that I don't have dreams and aspirations. I'm just not going to a D1 school on a full scholarship. I do okay at school, but I was never an academic whiz which is why I'm going to the local community college to be a court stenographer.

Ben is the anomaly in our small town. Hardly any of our class is going so far away. Most are attending state colleges, many will work on their family's ranches, or businesses. For me, my dad needs me to help out with Rowan and Koa. He has to work long hours at his job to support us and they're not old enough to be left on their own.

So, Ben will be leaving me and Willowbrook in his rearview mirror to start a life I can't imagine. He's going to experience new things, meet new people and eventually, I'm going to look like a used ragdoll compared to all the shiny new girls.

Which is why I'm determined to make today the best day ever.

We pull up to the area where everyone always parks and

there's already a decent amount of people. It's not unexpected, teenagers and college kids gather here all summer long.

The old quarry is the spot for the local young people to hang out without adult supervision. It's not like the adults don't know about this place, most of them hung out here when they were younger. Maybe that's the reason they leave us alone.

Ben parks and we both hop out of the car, me with the beach bag full of supplies. He's great for a lot of things, but preparation isn't one of them. If I relied on Ben to bring what we need, we'd be dehydrated and burnt by noon.

We approach the swimming hole and say hello to a few classmates but don't join them, instead veering off to the side to sit on our own.

The water surrounds us on three sides by tall rock walls and on the fourth side, where the land gently slopes into the water, is where everyone congregates. It's sandy there and I don't know if that's a naturally occurring thing or if someone trucked in sand at some point—it's just always been this way.

We spread the blanket and Ben's eyes flare with apprecia-tion when I strip off my sundress. *I need him to remember me like this.* Then I grab the sunscreen from the bag, squeeze a dollop into my palm and rub it on my legs, arms and chest.

"Can you rub sunscreen on my back?" I offer him the bottle.

Ben swallows, his Adam's apple bobbing. "Sure."

I lay face down on the blanket and Ben crawls over me, straddling my ass, being careful not to rest all his weight while he leans forward and rubs sunscreen on my skin.

"Love the bikini."

I chuckle. "You say that every time I wear it."

"Well, you look smokin' hot every time you wear it." His fingers work in the sunscreen over my back, ending with a light smack on my ass. He rolls over onto his back beside me on the blanket, staring up at the blue sky and bright sun.

"My turn." I scoot up onto my knees and grab the bottle of sunscreen, dispensing a generous amount into my palm. Ben shrugs off his T-shirt and uncaringly tosses it into the sand.

The space between my thighs tingles when his broad chest comes into view. There's a dusting of hair that leads from his belly button down below his shorts that always gets me hot.

I playfully straddle him and his hands move directly to my hips. My hands move over the rise and fall of his muscles, making sure sunscreen is covering every inch.

"You're giving me ideas," he says in a strained voice.

His growing bulge under my ass tells me exactly what kind of ideas he's having, but I play innocent.

"What kind would those be?"

Ben growls and I giggle. "You know exactly what you're doing."

"I don't know what you're talking about." I lean forward to slide the sunscreen over the top of his shoulders and place my mouth to his, making sure my breasts rub up along his chest.

He deepens the kiss and I lower my body on top of his.

"Ben! Gill! This is a public beach!" Our names are shouted across the space, echoing off the rock walls behind us.

Laughter ensues and we part, turning our heads in the direction of the voice. It's Brooks, Ben's best friend with a group of kids from our graduating class. Disappointment gnaws in my stomach because they're going to hang out with us and I'm feeling protective—I greedily want my last moments with Ben to be with him alone.

"Shit," Ben groans. "I gotta turn over so they don't see my hard-on." His cheeks are pink and I laugh, rolling off of him.

Ben and I have been together for years, but we only started

sleeping together at the beginning of our senior year. While Ben doesn't hold back when we're together, he always seems a little embarrassed whenever the subject of sex comes up in front of other people.

He rolls over and I straddle him again, this time sitting on his ass, applying the sunscreen to his back.

"Hey guys," I say when the group reaches us.

"You guys been here long?" Brooks asks. Although he played quarterback on the football team, he either didn't try to play in college or he just didn't have it because he's attending state.

"Nope, just got here." I climb off Ben and sit on the blanket beside him.

His hard-on must be gone because he rolls over. "You guys heading to my place later?"

"You know it," one of the other guys says.

"How could we not spend the fourth at Plain Daisy?" Brooks says. "Is Lottie going to be there?"

Ben glances at me. "She's my cousin, so yeah."

Brooks nods and looks around the quarry.

For the next hour the group talks mostly about where everyone's headed for college and how excited they all are. I'm one of the few staying in Willowbrook and when one of the girls asks if I'm looking forward to starting my classes, I feign excitement.

I'm excited to become a court stenographer. I just wish I were going to school in South Carolina with Ben. He's the north star in my life.

"I'm getting hot. Wanna swim babe?" Ben asks me.

Ben can always tell when I'm bothered or uncomfortable with others or their conversations.

He leans over and whispers in my ear. "C'mon. Let's go."

When he pulls back, his eyes hold the look. The one that

means he's horny. My nipples pebble in my bikini top, and Ben notices, licking his lips.

I hop up off the blanket and accept his outstretched hand. We run toward the water, Brooks shouting something obscene.

Chapter Three

BEN

The cool water feels good against my scorching skin on a hot day like today.

There are other kids in the water, a few of my teammates throwing a football around but when they ask me to join them, I decline.

Gillian was uncomfortable about the never-ending conversation with our friends about everyone moving on. I wish more than anything that she could come with me, but her family situation won't allow for her to leave. I worry she feels less than because I'm going to a four-year university and she's staying local. She should be proud of how selfless she's being by pitching in to take care of her siblings. Not everyone would do that. When your mom dies at five, you tend to see the importance of family. Then again, I'm abandoning mine.

"Think you can beat me to the other side of the quarry?" I grin.

She looks out at the distance. It's not that far, definitely swimmable but not easy. I'm a stronger swimmer only because my brothers, cousins and I spent a lot of our summer swimming in the lake smack-dab in the middle of Plain Daisy Ranch property.

We're standing at the edge of the drop off and the bottom of the quarry is like a cliff underwater about fifty feet from the edge. Once we start swimming to the other side there will be no place to stop and rest—leaving hundreds of feet between us and the bottom.

I want to get her mind off of me leaving, but I also have an ulterior motive.

"I'll give it my best shot." She takes off before I start to count down.

I laugh and push off the hard bottom, swimming forward. "Head toward that outcropping of rock."

The quarry is shaped like a sideways oval except for one area where there's a small outcropping of rock. The bottom is shallow enough for us to stand, and it's the one spot that offers any semblance of privacy.

The water grows cooler the further out we swim, but it's still refreshing and not numb inducing.

I lag behind, keeping Gillian ahead of me so I can keep an eye on her and make sure she's okay until we're close to a group of rocks. Once I know she'll reach it safely, I give it my all and easily swim past her until I reach the area where I can stand.

She approaches a few minutes later and I lean against a rock with my arms crossed and taunt her with a smirk. "I've been waiting here for ages."

Her eyes narrow, and I laugh. About thirty seconds later she reaches me, and my hands grab her hips and drag her to me.

"Just letting me think I could win, huh?"

I shrug. "Maybe."

She rolls her eyes and shakes her head. "Is there anything you're not good at?"

"English. Biology. Spanish." It's true. I'm not terrible but let's just say it's a good thing I snagged an athletic scholarship, otherwise I wouldn't be going to a school like Clemson.

"Join the club." Her mouth twists down.

"Hey." I push my hand into her wet hair. "You're gonna kill it in your courses this fall."

She looks away from my gaze. "Maybe. I'm sure as hell going to try. But it's not like I'm heading down the same path as you."

I frown. "Everyone has their own thing going on, their own road to go down. One isn't better than the other. The only thing that matters is you and I."

Gillian smiles and I lower my head, pressing my lips to hers. Her arms wrap around my neck, and she deepens the kiss this time. I'm gonna miss her so much. She has no idea how badly my heart aches thinking about not seeing her every day.

My cock grows rock hard in my wet swim trunks.

No surprise. I basically think and want to have sex with Gillian 24/7, but I don't want her to think all I want from her is to get laid. Especially today.

But I can't fight the struggle right now because her hard nipples are pressed into my chest through the thin fabric of her bikini top.

My breathing picks up and my hands graze down her body until they're both on her ass. I squeeze and lift her into my arms. Gillian wraps her legs around my waist and moans into my mouth when my hard length presses against her core.

Thankfully, there's still enough of my brain working for me to realize that we need to move further back behind the outcropping of rock so we're hidden from the people in the water and on the beach. I don't want to hear Brooks mouth when we get back.

We won't be completely out of view, but it's the best we can do.

I walk us backward until we're tucked behind the rock. There's a small ledge underwater and I sit down. I can't fuck Gillian right here without other people knowing, but there's other stuff we can do.

I pull away and her beauty strikes me. Her hooded eyes are dazed, holding that turned-on spark that I love.

Just like me.

"I want you so fucking bad right now, but I'm not going to do it where someone might see."

Her shoulders sag and disappointment paints her face.

"I have another idea though." I pull her a little closer. "Try to act like we're just having a conversation. My hand dips underwater and my fingers slide her bikini bottom to the side.

She's surrounded by water from her chest up, but my fingers coat her with the slickness between her thighs.

Her lips press together and she sucks in a long draw of air as I toy with her clit, massaging it slowly before sliding a finger further to her entrance. She gasps when I push a finger in and her head arches back.

"Careful babe. You gotta act like we're just talking remember? Otherwise, I'll have to stop."

Her head snaps up and she stares me down. "Don't you dare."

"That's better." I push another finger into her and her eyes drift closed. "Eyes open."

She opens them, her blue eyes killing me. A mischievous smile crosses her lips. "You think it's so easy?"

Her hand grips the rigid length of my cock that's bulging out of my swim trunks. I release a low groan and she grins, a satisfactory "I got you" smile. And when she forces the waistband of my swim trunks down so they're tucked under my balls I can barely hold back from leaning forward and devouring her. To hell with any onlookers.

The water is so high up on her body you can barely tell

that her arm is moving when she starts to jerk me off, sliding her thumb over the head each time she reaches it.

She strokes her hand down.

I have to force myself to concentrate to continue moving my fingers in and out of her. She has to get off, too, because there's no doubt that she's taking me to that barrier of no return.

I curve my fingers when they're inside of her just like I discovered she loved years ago in the cab of my Jeep in Hickory at our secret make out place. She squeals louder as always and her eyes float back under her eyelids. Her fingers grip me tighter, whether on purpose or not, I don't know, but I groan.

"Not so easy, is it?"

I lean in and kiss the smug look off her face, not caring if anyone witnesses us.

When I draw back, I grin and shift my thumb so that it rubs against her clit. The expression on her face is one of pain but I know that it's merely her begging for me to put her out of her misery and make her come.

I'm at the brink myself, so I increase the pressure and when her body flushes pink and she's grinding along my hand making it obvious she's a second from climax, I stop restraining myself and allow my orgasm to take over.

We come at the same time, making small noises but both of us pressing our lips together to trap the sound within ourselves. She's way more successful at hiding it than I am.

Afterward, we both heave for a breath and stare at each other. She's smiling at me with sun-kissed skin and a bright smile. As I've done with almost everything today, I commit this moment to memory. This is how I want to remember her as I lay in my twin bed living with a bunch of strangers. Satisfied, loved and happy.

It's not that I don't want out of this small town... I have the same itch most of my classmates have to discover the world. But this town is all I've ever known and thoughts of her are what's going to keep me going when it gets tough—and I have no doubt it will.

The football schedule is grueling, not to mention the schoolwork. I have to maintain a decent grade point average and if I don't, my dream crashes. And I'm committed to making it to the pros. Otherwise, I'll end up like Jude working on the ranch, without any hope to escape.

Living in Willowbrook isn't a bad life, it's just not one I ever saw myself having.

It's a good thing Gillian feels the same. That's how I know we'll make it. We'll graduate and when I get drafted into the pros, I'm coming back to ride her into the sunset in my new expensive sports car and million dollar check in my pocket.

Chapter Four

GILLIAN

God, that Ben's amazing. It takes me a moment to come out of the daze and realize that there's a lot of shouting and raucous laughter coming from the beach.

"What the hell is that about?" Ben says, moving further out from behind the outcropping of rock to check the noise out.

My vision follows his to find a bunch of people standing at the edge of the water, watching someone walk away. We're too far away for me to make out who the person is.

"Should we head back?" I ask.

I don't want to be out here alone with Ben too long, otherwise people will gossip about what we're doing. I'm not naïve, most of them either know or guess that we've messed around with each other after all these years. I just don't want to have to listen to everyone razz me about it for the rest of the summer after Ben's gone. Or think I'm some stupid girl who gave my virginity to a guy who is on to bigger and better things.

"Yeah, we probably should."

There's disappointment in his voice which I take as a good

sign. It must mean he'd rather stay here in our own little world with me.

We swim back, not nearly as fast as we came across the water. Once we're almost to the part where we can stand, I spot someone push through the shrubbery at the top of the rock wall of the quarry—someone very familiar.

"Is that Emmett?"

"What? Where?" Ben asks from behind me.

I tread water and point up at the top of the cliff.

Ben turns his head in the direction I point. "What the fuck?"

Emmett is standing at the top of Dead Man's Drop. A couple of decades ago, it's rumored that a teenager jumped from there and died. The police roped it off right after and in all the times I've swam here no one has dared to sneak up there to jump off.

"C'mon." Ben swims faster and I struggle to keep up, leaving me panting for breath by the time we reach where I can stand.

Now I see what all the fuss is about. Half the people are screaming at Emmett to quit playing around and come back down—mostly the girls, and the other half—the guys, are cajoling him on.

"Get your ass down here," Ben bellows across the water.

"Hey, bro!" Emmett waves like the immature idiot he is at times. If he wasn't such a teddy bear at heart, people wouldn't forgive him so fast on the stupid shit that comes out of his mouth.

"How the hell did he even get here?" Ben mutters under his breath. "Don't you dare fucking jump!" he scolds.

"What, like this?" He propels himself off the edge.

An audible gasp erupts from the crowd as his body sails down from the cliff. My hands fly up to my mouth, bile rises up my throat. My eyes don't stray, fixated on his body freefalling through the air. Time slows as he's suspended, the seconds feeling like hours.

He straightens out his body, dropping into the water, causing a giant splash. My breathing lodges in my throat, as we all wait in silence for his head to pop up to the surface.

Out the three Noughton boys, Emmett is the crazy one. Jude is the responsible one, and Ben is the athletic one. Emmett loves to buck the system and holds a wild side to him that gets him in trouble. The people around Willowbrook like to say that if Emmett had been born first, they would've been coined the Naughty boys rather than the Noughton boys. But risking his life just to put on a show for the people is taking his rebellious nature too far.

When Emmett doesn't surface after a few seconds, I glance at Ben and see him step forward, ready to dive in after him. Emmett breaks through the surface, but he's floating face up in the water.

"Oh my god!" I cry out.

Ben dives in, swimming in his brother's direction as everyone whispers to one another. Tears spring to my eyes. The Noughton family cannot take another loss, they've never fully gotten over their mother dying.

"Emmett! Emmett!" Ben screams.

He's inches away when Emmett's eyes spring open and the lower half of his body sinks into the water. His laughter echoing through the warm air.

Ben's back is facing me, but he stops swimming and treads water. The muscles in his back flex and he splashes water at his brother's face.

"What the fuck?" Ben shouts.

"Relax, I'm just playing around." Emmett holds his usual carefree facial expression, not the least bit concerned that he just scared the shit out of everyone.

I don't know how he manages, but Ben stays afloat and

cocks his fist, landing a hard hit on his brother's face. "You ever fucking do that again and I'll beat the shit outta you!"

Emmett cringes in pain, his hand holding his eye. Ben swims toward shore. I scowl at Emmett and follow Ben, meeting him on the beach.

"You okay?" I ask in a low voice, my hand on his forearm.

"He's so fucking stupid." He flops himself down on the blanket.

"You want a beer man?" Brooks asks, opening the cooler snug in the sand next to him.

"Nah, I'm driving."

A flash of panic tightens my chest. It's already time to head to Plain Daisy Ranch? I silently wish time would slow down.

We lay down to let the heated rays of sun dry us off. My nerves are just calming down when a hand clamps around mine. I open my eyes, turning my head to the side to shield the sun.

"We should get going." Ben's eyes hold regret, like he's sorry we have to leave already because this will be our last time here as a couple together for who knows how long, maybe forever.

Sure, I'll be back at some point with my friends, but not with Ben.

I nod and gather our things. I'm just putting the sunscreen back in the bag when Emmett approaches us with a sheepish look.

"Can I get a lift back with you guys?" he asks.

"Yep." Ben nods at him toward the truck.

Ben would never hold a grudge or fight with his brothers for any extended period of time. One of the things I love about him is how he knows how much family means.

"See you guys later," I say to the others on our way out.

Everyone says their goodbyes and tells us that they'll see us at Ben's family ranch later.

I sit between Ben and Emmett on the way home as they each keep changing the stations, bickering over the radio. Each one fighting the other for control. I'm filled with a sense of nostalgia I don't quite understand because it's happening in real time, but it almost feels as though I'm living out a memory, I'll miss some day.

But that can't be right. There's many more of these rides down the dirt roads with the warm breeze blowing through the cab of the truck to come in our future. There has to be. We have our plan. Ben goes to Clemson and once he gets drafted, we reunite. If only that feeling in my gut that says I'm a naïve teenager who thinks she met her soul mate way too young would disappear.

❧

THE FIRST THING I DO WHEN WE GET TO BEN'S IS change my clothes. I purposely wore the cornflower blue sundress dress because it's Ben's favorite. He loves the way it matches the color of my eyes.

After I leave my bag in Ben's room I head to the kitchen. Ben, Jude, and Bruce all look in my direction when I enter. The first time I came here as Ben's girlfriend his dad insisted that I call him Bruce and not Mr. Noughton, something that took a while to stick with me.

"How're you doing, darlin'?" Bruce wraps his arm around my shoulders, giving me a side hug.

I've seen him rip up one side and down the other of his sons, but he's always treated me with care and been extra sweet.

"I'm good. How about you?"

"Just talkin' to my boys about this one leaving tomorrow. You all set to see him do big things at Clemson?" One thing about Bruce, his proudness of Ben is always transparent on his face.

When I glance at Ben, he shifts his weight and stares down to the floor. He's always a little uncomfortable when his dad sings his praises, but he should be overjoyed. He's worked hard to get where he's going.

Jude is his usual stoic self, watching on silently, always observing the room.

"He's going to be great." I walk over to Ben and wrap my arms around his middle. He leans down and kisses the top of my head. "Can I help with anything before everyone gets here?"

"Was hoping I could talk you into making that potato salad that's so good while the boys and I set up outside."

I smile. "Of course, I can." I made my late mom's recipe last year for the fourth and Bruce asked me to make it a bunch more times during the year. Her recipes are one of the few things she left me and I always feel close to her whenever I make one of her specialties.

"I already boiled the potatoes last night. They're in the fridge."

Pulling away from Ben, I head over to the fridge. "Careful Bruce, people are going to call you domesticated if you're not careful."

Bruce lets loose a big, belly laugh.

"I don't think anyone would ever accuse him of that," Jude says.

The whole room erupts into laughter. After being a widower for so many years, he's still doesn't separate the darks from the whites, causing the boys white socks to turn pink.

The guys head outside while I assemble what I need for the potato salad. Everyone who comes, brings a side dish— usually the same thing year after year. Mrs. Webster always bakes a blueberry pie with stars cut out on the top and Mrs.

Fortmeyer brings a giant batch of her chili that won at the state fair two years running.

I chuckle to myself as I cut up the potatoes, wondering whether I'll be known for this potato salad in thirty years. Ben's wife, Gillian Noughton makes her famous potato salad, I dream to myself. If they come true that is.

A part of me hopes so, but that would mean staying in this town when I intend to be by Ben's side wherever he's playing football once I'm finished school and my siblings are older.

Only one of those destinies can come true and I hope it's the later.

Chapter Five

BEN

People trickle onto the ranch a couple hours after the parade in Willowbrook's downtown is finished. At first, it's mostly the older people in town and the families with small children, but later my brothers' and my friends show up.

By the time the pig is done roasting, people are scattered everywhere all over the ranch. The little ones run rampant, some of them with smeared spiderman and rainbows painted on their faces. Teenagers are playing cornhole while the senior citizens are content to sit in a circle, beers in hand, relaying stories they've all told and heard a hundred times.

I'm stuck talking to Mr. Wilson who's telling me all about the gout in his foot when my dad approaches. Thank God. I need someone to give me an excuse to stop talking to Mr. Wilson—everyone in town knows that he can somehow weave a tale about the most mundane thing and make it last an hour.

"Hey, John." My dad nods in greeting and turns his attention to me. "You seen Emmett around?"

I shake my head. "Nah, haven't seen him in a while."

"Go find him. I promised some of the littles a trot on Meadow and Lark."

They're our two ponies that won't scare the little kids too much.

"I'll go see if I can track him down."

I scan the area and Gillian is still chatting with some of her friends over by the food table, so I head off in search of Emmett. My dad could ask me to lead the ponies around while all the little kids take a turn riding them, but Emmett's been a natural with them since they arrived.

At first, the ponies were skittish and nervous but as soon as Emmett went in the pen, they relaxed. Which is pretty weird given that my little brother doesn't exude what one might call calming energy. He's always busting at the seams with chaotic energy.

I search through everyone who's lingering outside and socializing in different groups, then I look in the house and finally I end up circling the barn, but he's nowhere to be found.

Where the hell could he have gone?

There's no reason for him to be in the barn, but I decide to check in there since there isn't anywhere left to check. He has an old dirt bike he fixed up that he sometimes rips around the property on and I want to make sure it's still there. Though I doubt I would've missed the sound of his muffler, even with the crowd and the music.

I slide the old barn door open a sliver for me to slide through and the first thing I see is the dirt bike, so that theory is a bust. I'm about to leave when I hear something almost like a muffled giggle, so I investigate.

When I round the corner of hay bales, Emmett hands are up the shirt of the preacher's daughter and his tongue down her throat. Neither of them notices me and their mouths keep tangling.

"Kimmie, your dad is looking for you."

Her head snaps away from my brother's and she stares at

me with wide eyes. Without a word she pushes against Emmett's chest, who staggers back a step, and rushes out of the barn.

I pin my brother with a stare. "Preacher Callaghan would have your balls if he saw what I just did."

He laughs and adjusts his dick in his pants. "That wouldn't be very godly of him."

"Why do you insist on making the worst choices?" First the cliff earlier today where he almost killed himself and now the preacher's daughter. There are a lot of girls who would have made out with him. He didn't have to choose the off-limits one.

Something flashes over his face. It's so quick that I almost miss it.

My eyes narrow. "What's going on?"

"Nothing. Let's go snatch some beers." He pushes past me but I place a hand on his chest and nudge him back.

"Bullshit. What is it?"

He studies me for a beat, gaze roaming my face like he's not sure whether he wants to admit whatever it is on his mind.

"Tell me."

With a deep sigh he pushes his hand through the waves on top of his head. "It's gonna be different without you here." He shrugs like it's no big deal but I realize that to him, my leaving is a bigger deal than I assumed it was. I've selfishly been thinking of myself and Gillian the last few weeks.

I don't know why I didn't think of it earlier. I've been so wrapped up in being nervous to move somewhere new and reassuring Gillian that we're going to be okay that I didn't stop to think about how Emmett might feel.

Jude will be fine, he's solid and stronger than I'll ever be, but Emmett has always used his humor and affable nature to push his feelings back.

"I'm gonna miss you, too," I say.

"Yeah, right." He pushes his hands into the pockets of his worn-out jeans. "You're gonna be off being a football god. You're gonna forget about this place."

"This place is all I've ever known."

"Whatever."

He tries to walk past me again, but I step in his way and do something I haven't done since we were little kids. I pull him into a hug, smacking him on the back.

"I'm gonna miss you. You need me, you call, all right?" Sometimes I forget that Emmett is a few years younger than Jude and me.

For a second I think he might push me away but he squeezes me tight. "Gonna miss you too."

There's an awkward beat when we separate for a moment, but then we both sort of laugh and walk out of the barn.

"I almost forgot. Dad wants you to walk some of the kids around on the ponies. That's why I came to find you."

I expect him to complain, but instead he nods and smiles. "Yeah, they'll probably like that. See you later." He peels off and heads in the direction of the horses while I come to a stop and look around.

Since I didn't realize I needed to have a conversation with Emmett before I left, I figure maybe I need to have one with Jude, too. I spot him standing off to the side of the crowd—no surprise there—with Sadie Wilkins. Also, not a surprise.

She's from the ranch that borders ours and is the same age as Jude. They've been best friends for as long as I can remember. Sadie seems to be about the only one who can put up with Jude's grumpy ways on the regular, though I don't know how she does it.

I head off in their direction.

"She just seems off. I don't know," I hear Sadie say as I approach.

"I can swing by tomorrow and have a look at her if you want," Jude says.

"That would be great. You're the best." She reaches out and squeezes his forearm and he sips his beer causing her hand to drop.

It always surprises me that these two never got together—at least as far as I know.

"Hey guys," I say.

Sadie smiles and tucks her blonde hair behind her ear.

Jude's eyebrows draw in like maybe he's annoyed that I'm here.

"What are you guys doing?" I ask.

"Nothing," Jude says.

"Just chatting," Sadie adds. "Are you excited to be leaving tomorrow?"

"Yeah. A little nervous though."

"That's normal. You're going to do amazing there. I know it." She leans in and gives me a hug.

"Thanks, Sadie."

Sadie has always been more like the sister that I never had than a neighbor to me, probably because of how much she was around when we were growing up.

"Do you mind if I talk to Jude for a second?"

"Not at all. I was just going to check out the food table. I'm getting hungry."

I give her a thankful smile before she turns and disappears into the crowd.

"What's this about?" Jude tilts his beer to his lips.

"Just wanted to touch base with you before tomorrow. Say thanks for helping Dad with the ranch and picking up my slack." I've never been as involved in ranch life as my two brothers but I do have some jobs that one or both of them have to take over now that I'm leaving.

"What else would I do?" He scowls.

Sometimes I think that maybe Jude resents that I'm so good at football. He played in high school but never looked into going anywhere after. Said he wasn't into it anymore. He was a solid player, but he wouldn't be going to college on any scholarships.

But Jude is just generally a grumpy guy, so it's hard to determine whether his attitude is directed at me specifically or life in general.

I push my hands into my pockets and shrug. "I don't know. I'm just saying."

"Listen, you go do your thing and do it well. Make something of yourself. Get drafted, have a long career in the pros and if you're lucky, you won't ever have to come back here."

I frown. "It's not like I'll never be back."

He steps up and clamps me on the shoulder, his matching brown eyes landing on mine. "If you're smart you won't be." He walks past me and leaves me standing on the outside of the crowd. For the first time, staring at what I'm leaving behind, I get a sense that I don't fit in this town anymore.

It's like one brother is afraid I'm going to forget all about this place and the other is afraid I won't.

Chapter Six

GILLIAN

I sip my beer and laugh at something Brooks says.

All of us teenagers are hiding behind the barn drinking the beer we managed to steal out of the coolers.

Well, all of us except for Ben. He took off like half an hour ago and hasn't returned. I keep glancing around hoping to spot him. The only reason I haven't gone in search of him is because I don't want to look like a psycho stalker, but our remaining hours together are whittling down.

I take another sip of my beer in an attempt to ease my frustrations. I've always been a lightweight, so I already feel the couple of beers I've consumed going to my head.

A hand on my waist draws my attention and I look to my side.

My body relaxes, my shoulders settling somewhere that isn't up by my ears.

He leans down and whispers, running his thumb along the inside of my wrist at the same time. "Mind if I steal you away?"

I turn and smile. "Not even a little."

He entwines our hands and sweeps me away from everyone. No one really seems to notice. They've all been drinking and are too involved in their own conversations.

"Where are we going?" I ask once we're far enough away from everyone.

"You'll see."

He leads me over to the drive shed they have and points to the UTV. "Hop in."

"What are you up to?" I give him a suspicious look.

"I told you, you'll see." He places a quick kiss on my lips. "Now get in."

I do as he says and within a minute he's inside and belted in. He takes off away from the party. We drive for five minutes and the sounds of the party drift farther and farther away until we can't hear the music or loud conversations anymore.

Ben follows one of the paths on the ranch until we reach the area that has a small river running toward the lake that sits in the middle of their property. It takes me a moment to realize what I'm looking at.

There's a blanket set up on the ground along with two pillows and another blanket on top. Flameless tea lights are placed all around the blanket casting an orange glow while the sound of the trickling river sounds around us. It's pure romantic.

"You did all this?" I ask him.

He nods. "Wanted you to myself before the night is over."

I rise to my tiptoes to kiss him, deepening the kiss but he pulls away.

"Let's not get too carried away yet." He chuckles and climbs out of the UTV, walking around to my side to help me out before leading me over to the blanket by the hand. "Thought we could star gaze."

I squeeze his hand. This is something we do when we want to be alone. His house is always bustling with his brothers and mine isn't an option to be alone because usually if I'm there it means I'm looking after my younger siblings.

We settle onto the blanket, lying side by side with our heads on the pillow. Ben pulls the blanket over us. It's not cold but this far from everyone else out in the open plains it's a little chillier. Besides, even if it weren't, I'll never complain about cuddling with Ben under a blanket.

We're joined by the hand, staring up at the sky for a few minutes when I think about how this is the last time we'll do this. Secretly, I hope it's the last time this summer and not ever. I'm going to miss him so much.

In many ways, Ben is my happiness. It's not that I don't want to help with my siblings—I love them more than anything. There are times I wish that I could just be a regular girl who comes and goes as she pleases. Mostly, one who was leaving for college. Preferably to South Carolina.

It's hard not to feel like everyone else around me is moving on with their lives, while I'm standing still watching.

"I just saw a shooting star. Did you see it?" Ben's voice says in the darkness.

I nod because I'm still trying to collect myself after the direction my thoughts have taken.

His weight shifts and he rolls over the top of me, looking down. "Gill, what's going on in that head of yours?" he asks in a soft voice.

I smile through the tears building in my eyes.

When I don't say anything, he bends down and kisses my forehead, resting his lips there for a moment. "We are going to be fine," he says against my skin and pulls back so I see the soft glow of the tealights on his face.

I'm not afraid Ben's going to run off to college and hook up with a bunch of different girls. He's not that kind of guy. But people grow apart and I'm worried that as soon as he sees what the rest of the world has to offer, he's not going to be interested in anything or anyone Willowbrook has to offer.

"Just promise me that if you feel your feelings toward me changing, that you'll talk to me about it."

He shakes his head before my sentence is complete. "That's not going to happen."

"Promise me." He meets my gaze.

"I promise, but that's not going to happen. You're the one for me. Part of the reason I'm doing this is for us. So that I can give you the life you deserve."

"I only want you." I place my hand on his cheek and he bends down and kisses me.

The kiss starts innocent enough but morphs into one of desperation and need. Soon my hands are in his hair and his hard length is pressing into my thigh. Before I know it, we're both stripped of our clothes, he's put on a condom and he's hovering above me, the stars glimmering over his shoulders.

"You have my word that I will always love you, Gill. No matter what." He eases inside of me.

I moan on an exhale and wrap my arms around him, pulling him to me until my breasts are pressed against his hard chest. My face rests on his neck as he slowly draws himself in and out, and my nipples harden.

Ben grunts and pulls back to stare into my eyes.

Our gazes lock as he makes love to me. At moments our lips meet but we never kiss for long, preferring instead to watch one another.

Everything he's said to me over the past several weeks is alive in his eyes. Every promise, every declaration, every oath.

Tears gather once again in my eyes but not out of fear or sadness, but from joy.

Ben rolls us over on the blanket so that I'm on top and I circle my hips. It feels freeing straddling him naked and having my chest exposed to the night air.

He reaches up and thumbs a nipple, then the other one as I move on top of him.

Soon the tingling at the apex of my thighs is so insistent that I can't ignore it and I begin grinding myself down on him.

Ben's half-lidded gaze takes me in and he smiles, a private smile that makes me want to know what his thoughts are.

I'm so close. Just a couple more...

I come on a cry, jerking my pelvis against Ben until the blissful sensation washes itself away.

Then Ben is back on top of me, thrusting in and out of me until he stills inside me, emptying himself into the condom.

He kisses me one final time before pulling out of me and sitting up to take it off. He collapses onto his back. I roll into him, and he wraps his muscled arm around me.

We lay with our bodies tangled together in the afterglow of making love. I feel closer to him in this moment than I probably ever have and suddenly, I no longer feel nervous for him to leave me. I know he loves me with his whole heart and though it may be rough at times, we're going to make it to the other side.

The fireworks from the party start and we both sit up, wrapping the blanket around our naked bodies to watch the colors explode in the night sky.

I commit this moment to memory so on the nights when I'm feeling lonely and wishing he were here, I'm going to remember this feeling I have now and remind myself that it will all work out.

"I love you," I whisper into the darkness.

"I love you. Always."

He cups my face and kisses me until I feel all his love pour out of him and into me. This is how it was meant to be. This is how it will always be between us, no matter what.

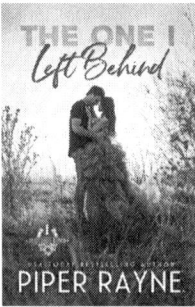

Do Ben and Gillian's relation-ship survive the distance? Find out in The One I Left Behind, the first full-length novel in our Plain Daisy Ranch series!

The One I Left Behind is available now.
Visit our website www.piperrayne.com

Also by Piper Rayne

My Vegas Groom

A Greene Family Summer Bash (Novella)

My Sister's Flirty Friend

My Unexpected Surprise

My Famous Frenemy

A Greene Family Vacation (Novella)

My Scorned Best Friend

My Fake Fiancé

My Brother's Forbidden Friend

A Greene Family Christmas (Novella)

Lake Starlight

The Problem with Second Chances

The Issue with Bad Boy Roommates

The Trouble with Runaway Brides

The Drawback of Single Dads

Modern Love

Charmed by the Bartender

Hooked by the Boxer

Mad about the Banker

Single Dads Club

Real Deal

Dirty Talker

Sexy Beast

Hollywood Hearts

Mister Mom

Animal Attraction

Domestic Bliss

Bedroom Games

Cold as Ice

On Thin Ice

Break the Ice

Chicago Law

Smitten with the Best Man

Tempted by my Ex-Husband

Seduced by my Ex's Divorce Attorney

Blue Collar Brothers

Flirting with Fire

Crushing on the Cop

Engaged to the EMT

White Collar Brothers

Sexy Filthy Boss

Dirty Flirty Enemy

Wild Steamy Hook-up

The Rooftop Crew

My Bestie's Ex

A Royal Mistake

The Rival Roomies

Our Star-Crossed Kiss

The Do-Over

A Co-Workers Crush

Hockey Hotties

Countdown to a Kiss (Free Prequel)

My Lucky #13 (FREE)

The Trouble with #9

Faking it with #41

Tropical Hat Trick (Novella)

Sneaking around with #34

Second Shot with #76

Offside with #55

Kingsmen Football Stars

False Start (Free Prequel)

You Had Your Chance, Lee Burrows

You Can't Kiss the Nanny, Brady Banks

Over My Brother's Dead Body, Chase Andrews

Chicago Grizzlies

On the Defense (Free Prequel)

Something like Hate

Something like Lust

Something like Love

Holiday Romances

Single and Ready to Jingle

Claus and Effect

About Piper & Rayne

Piper Rayne is a USA Today Bestselling Author duo who write "heartwarming humor with a side of sizzle" about families, whether that be blood or found. They both have e-readers full of one-clickable books, they're married to husbands who drive them to drink, and they're both chauffeurs to their kids. Most of all, they love hot heroes and quirky heroines who make them laugh, and they hope you do, too!

Printed in Great Britain
by Amazon

51800757R00029